THIS BOOK BELONGS TO:

_____

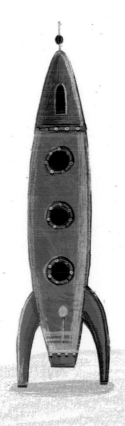

FOR OLIVIA, WITH LOVE BEYOND WORDS
– K.C.

TO JAN AND LENKA D.
– K.L.

This paperback edition first published in Great Britain in 2019 by Andersen Press Ltd.,
20 Vauxhall Bridge Road, London SW1V 2SA.
Text copyright © 2018 by Kathryn Cristaldi
Illustrations copyright © 2018 by Kristyna Litten
Published by arrangement with HarperCollins Publishers,. New York, NY, 10007 USA.
The rights of Kathryn Cristaldi and Kristyna Litten to be identified as the author and
illustrator of this work have been asserted by them in accordance
with the Copyright, Designs and Patents Act, 1988.
All rights reserved.
Printed and bound in China.
1   3   5   7   9   10   8   6   4   2
British Library Cataloguing in Publication Data available.
ISBN 978 1 78344 836 4

I'll Love You...

KATHRYN CRISTALDI KRISTYNA LITTEN

Andersen Press

I will love you till the cows come home

from a trip to Mars through skies unknown in a rocket ship made of glass and stone.

I will love you till the cows come home.

I will love you till the yaks come back
from a jaunt to town for a grassy snack

in a fire truck...

or a
Cadillac.

I will love you till the
yaks come back.

I will love you till the sheep set sail

on a cruise ship bound
for the Isle of Kale,

past manatees

and a humpback whale.

I will love you till the sheep set sail.

I will love you till the wolves
return from a bumpy ride
over rocks and fern,

the pigs all shouting
with concern.

I will love you till the
wolves return.

I will love you till the frogs ride past

on big-wheeled bikes going superfast...

in a circus for sea horses,
shrimp
and bass.

I will love you till the frogs ride past.

I will love you till the deer dance by
from a tap contest under the blue sky,

with a prize of clover and twig pot pie.
I will love you till the deer dance by.

I will love you till the geese flap down

to a warm ski lodge in a snowy town
with gourmet marshmallows, chocolaty brown.

I will love you till the geese flap down.

I will love you till the ants march in

wearing tiny ant hats
and tiny ant grins

and birthday cake crumbs on their tiny ant chins.
I will love you till the ants march in.

I'll love you till then, and again and again,
till my love makes a bed for the cows in their pen

and the yaks

and the sheep

and the wolves settle in,

and the frogs softly strum
on their frog violins,